The Magic School Bus
Inside the Human Body

By Joanna Cole   Illustrated by Bruce Degen

SCHOLASTIC INC.
New York Toronto London Auckland Sydney

The author and illustrator wish to thank Dr. Arnold J. Capute,
Associate Professor of Pediatrics, Director, Division of Child Development,
Johns Hopkins University School of Medicine, for his help in preparing this book.

ISBN 0-590-41427-5

Text copyright © 1989 by Joanna Cole.
Illustrations copyright © 1989 by Bruce Degen.
All rights reserved. Published by Scholastic Inc.
MAGIC SCHOOL BUS is a trademark of Scholastic Inc.

20 19 18 17 16   2 3 4 5/9

YOUR BODY IS MADE OF CELLS
by Rachel

Your body seems to be all one piece, but actually it is made of trillions of tiny pieces, called cells.

MY BODY IS MADE OF *TRILLIONS* OF CELLS.

SO IS MINE!

The very next day, The Friz made us do an experiment on our own bodies.

SEE *YOUR OWN* CELLS

Most cells are so small that we can't see them without a microscope.

① Gently scrape inside of cheek with toothpick

② Stir end of toothpick in drop of water on a slide.

③ Add a drop of Iodine Solution to color cells.

④ Look at slide under microscope. See Your cells.

OOOH, WEIRD!

Then she announced that we were going on a class trip to the science museum. We were going to see an exhibit about how our bodies get energy from the food we eat.

YOUR CELLS NEED ENERGY TO HELP YOU GROW, MOVE, TALK, THINK, AND PLAY.

Jail cell

JUST BEING IN MS. FRIZZLE'S CLASS TAKES ALL MY ENERGY.

DIFFERENT KINDS OF CELLS HAVE DIFFERENT JOBS
by Gregory

Lung cells help you breathe.

Muscle cells help you move.

ODE TO JELLY

Brain cells help you think.

The trip started out like any other trip.
We rode to the museum
in the old school bus.
Along the way,
we stopped at a park for lunch.

When it was time to go,
everyone got back on the bus—
everyone but Arnold.
He was still at the picnic table,
daydreaming and eating
a bag of Cheesie-Weesies.

WHEN YOU EAT, YOUR BODY <u>DIGESTS</u> THE FOOD SO YOUR CELLS CAN USE IT TO MAKE ENERGY.

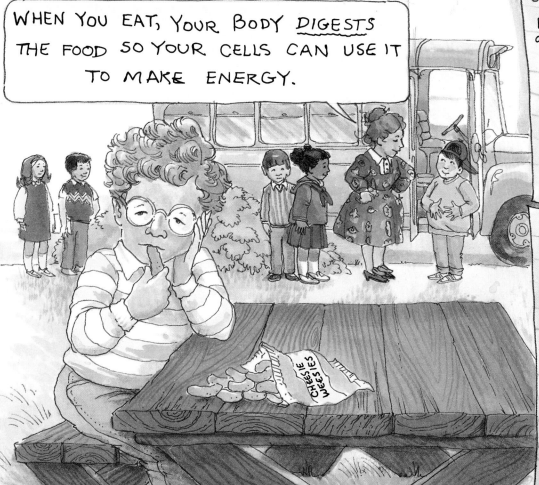

YOUR BODY NEEDS GOOD FOOD
by Carmen
For high energy and good growing power eat lots of:

Fresh fruits and Vegetables

Milk and Milk products

Whole grain Cereal and Pasta

Lean Meats, fish, Poultry, AND eggs

AND <u>NOT</u> TOO MUCH JUNK FOOD!

A SCIENCE WORD
by Dorothy Ann

<u>Digestion</u> comes from a word that means to divide. When food is digested it is divided into smaller and smaller parts.

"Hurry up, Arnold!" called Ms. Frizzle. She reached for the ignition key, but instead she pushed a strange little button nearby.

At once, we started shrinking and spinning through the air.

From inside, we couldn't see what was happening. All we knew was that we landed suddenly...

and then we were going down a dark tunnel.
We had no idea where we were.
But, as usual, Ms. Frizzle knew.
She said we were inside a human body,
going down the esophagus—
the tube that leads from the throat
to the stomach.
Most of us were too upset
about leaving Arnold behind
to pay much attention.

WHERE'S ARNOLD?

HE GOT LEFT!

THAT'S WHAT HAPPENS WHEN YOU EAT JUNK FOOD!

I THOUGHT WE WERE GOING TO THE MUSEUM.

THERE'S BEEN A SLIGHT CHANGE OF PLANS... WE'RE BEING DIGESTED INSTEAD.

FOOD GOES TO YOUR STOMACH THROUGH THE ESOPHAGUS
by Wanda
The food does not just fall down.
It is pushed along by muscle actions the way toothpaste is squeezed out of a tube. That's why you can swallow even when you are upside down.

MUSCLES SQUEEZE TO PUSH FOOD TO YOUR STOMACH

WHY ARE THE INTESTINES COILED UP?
by John

In an adult the intestines are 7.5 meters (25 feet) long. If they were stretched out straight, a person would have to be as tall as a house.

STOMACH

FOOD GOES FROM THE STOMACH TO THE SMALL INTESTINE

WASTE GOES OUT THROUGH THE LARGE INTESTINE

The small intestine was
a coiled-up hollow tube.
The inner walls of the tube were covered
with tiny "fingers" called *villi*.
"In the *villi* are tiny blood vessels.
Food molecules are taken into
these blood vessels,"
said Ms. Frizzle.
"Once the food is in the blood,
it can travel all over the body."

We felt ourselves getting even smaller,
and Ms. Frizzle started driving
into one of the *villi*.
She was going straight into a blood vessel!

BLOOD GOES ROUND
AND ROUND
        by Michael
In less than a minute
your blood makes
a trip all around
your body.
    This is called the
circulation of the
blood.

ONE MORE SCIENCE WORD
        by Dorothy Ann
Circulate comes from
a word that means
"to circle". Blood
Circulates - circles -
all around your body.

From the lungs, our red blood cells
carried us back to the heart.
This time we were on the left side
of the heart—the side that pumps
fresh blood back to the body again.
"Kids, it looks as if these red
blood cells are on their way to
the brain," said Ms. Frizzle.

LOOK! WHEN THE
RED BLOOD CELLS
PICK UP OXYGEN, THEY
TURN BRIGHT RED.

FROM RIGHT LUN

AIR
SAC

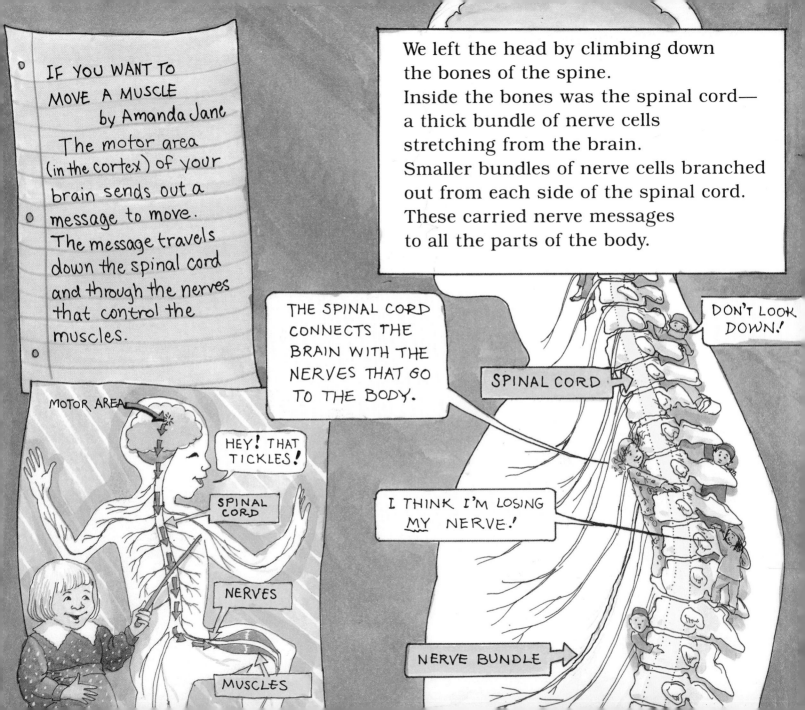

We followed some nerves that went to the leg muscles.
The leg muscles were working hard.
They needed a lot of energy.
They used up a lot of food and oxygen from the blood.
The heart was beating faster to carry fresh blood to the muscle cells.

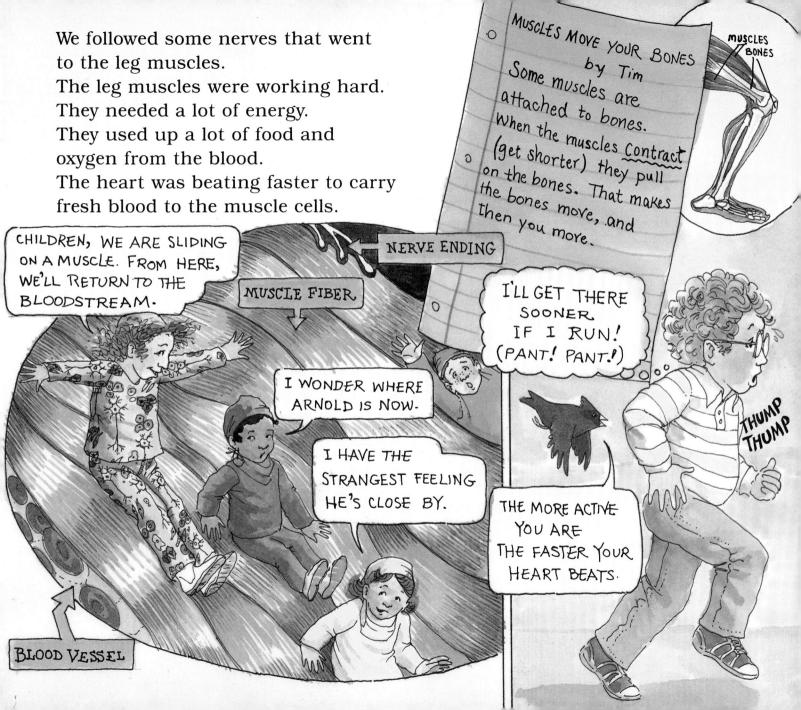

MUSCLES MOVE YOUR BONES
by Tim
Some muscles are attached to bones. When the muscles contract (get shorter) they pull on the bones. That makes the bones move, and then you more.

MUSCLES
BONES

CHILDREN, WE ARE SLIDING ON A MUSCLE. FROM HERE, WE'LL RETURN TO THE BLOODSTREAM.

NERVE ENDING

MUSCLE FIBER

I'LL GET THERE SOONER IF I RUN! (PANT! PANT!)

I WONDER WHERE ARNOLD IS NOW.

I HAVE THE STRANGEST FEELING HE'S CLOSE BY.

THE MORE ACTIVE YOU ARE THE FASTER YOUR HEART BEATS.

THUMP THUMP

BLOOD VESSEL

When we emerged from the bloodstream,
we were in a huge open space.
"Where are we?" asked a kid.
Ms. Frizzle explained,
"Children, this is the nasal cavity."
"The what?" we asked.
"The inside of the nose," said The Friz.
Suddenly, we heard a deafening noise.
It sounded like "Ah-aa-aa-ah!"

A tremendous blast of air
hit the bus full force.
We flew forward,
spinning around and around.

CHILDREN, PREPARE
FOR LANDING.
PLEASE REMAIN SEATED
UNTIL THE SCHOOL BUS
HAS COME TO A
COMPLETE STOP.

IS SHE FOR REAL?

A-A-A-AH
CHOO!

GESUNDHEIT!

We were going so fast,
we couldn't see anything,
but we could tell we were getting bigger.
Then—thud!—we landed.
There we were, back at school.
And there was Arnold,
in the school parking lot,
blowing his nose.

"Arnold!" we said, "the trip was *amazing!*
You should have been there!"

Back in the classroom, it was business as usual. Ms. Frizzle made us draw a chart of the human body for the bulletin board.

THE KIDNEYS CLEAN YOUR BLOOD AND MAKE URINE.

THE BLADDER STORES URINE.

KIDNEYS

BLADDER

LIVER

STOMACH

THE LIVER STORES VITAMINS AND DESTROYS POISONS. IT ALSO MAKES BILE, A FLUID THAT HELPS DIGEST FATTY FOODS.

NERVE

BLOOD VESSEL

BONE

MUSCLE

TRUE-OR-FALSE TEST

STOP! TAKE THIS TEST!
DO NOT WATCH T.V. ... YET.
DO NOT GET A SNACK... YET.
DO NOT PLAY A VIDEO
GAME ... YET.

FIRST TAKE THIS TEST.

HOW TO:
Read the sentences below. Decide if each one is true or false. To see if you are correct, check the answers on the opposite page.

QUESTIONS:

1. A school bus can enter someone's body and kids can go on a tour. True or false?

2. Museums are boring. True or false?

3. Arnold should not have tried to get back to school by himself. True or false?

4. Children cannot breathe or talk when they are surrounded by a liquid. True or false?

5. If the children really were as small as cells, we couldn't see them without a microscope. True or false?

6. White blood cells actually chase and destroy disease germs. True or false?

7. Ms. Frizzle really knew where Arnold was the whole time. True or false?

ANSWERS:

1. False! That could not happen in real life. (Not even to Arnold.)

   But in this story the author had to make it happen. Otherwise, the book would have been about a trip to a museum, instead of a trip through the body.

2. False! Museums are interesting and fun. But they are not as weird and gross as actually going inside a human body.

3. True! In real life, it would have been safer if Arnold had found a police officer to help.

4. True. If children were *really* inside a blood vessel, they would drown. It must have been magic.

5. True! The pictures in this book show the cells and the children greatly enlarged.

6. True! As unbelievable as it seems, real white blood cells actually behave just like the ones in this book. They even squeeze through the cells of blood vessel walls to capture germs in your organs and tissues.

7. Probably true. No one is absolutely sure, but most people think Ms. Frizzle knows *everything*.

PLEASE DO NOT WRITE IN THIS BOOK.

THANK YOU.